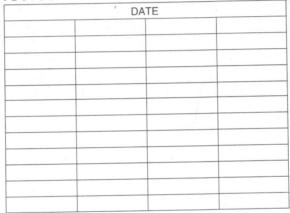

DIPUCCHI   DiPucchio, Kelly S.
O
           Gilbert Goldfish
           wants a pet.

MAY   2015

                    32026002643747

$16.99

DATE			

Gilbert Goldfish Wants a Pet

by **Kelly DiPucchio** illustrated by **Bob Shea**

Dial Books for Young Readers an imprint of Penguin Young Readers Group

For Dad, Bea, and The Seestadt Kids—
Austin, Alec, Olivia, Sebastian, and Gabriella
—K. D.

For Laura
—B. S.

DIAL BOOKS FOR YOUNG READERS
A division of Penguin Young Readers Group
Published by The Penguin Group
Penguin Group (USA) Inc., 375 Hudson Street, New York, NY 10014, U.S.A.
Penguin Group (Canada), 90 Eglinton Avenue East, Suite 700,
Toronto, Ontario, Canada M4P 2Y3 (a division of Pearson Penguin Canada Inc.)
Penguin Books Ltd, 80 Strand, London WC2R 0RL, England
Penguin Ireland, 25 St. Stephen's Green, Dublin 2, Ireland (a division of Penguin Books Ltd)
Penguin Group (Australia), 250 Camberwell Road, Camberwell, Victoria 3124, Australia
(a division of Pearson Australia Group Pty Ltd)
Penguin Books India Pvt Ltd, 11 Community Centre, Panchsheel Park, New Delhi - 110 017, India
Penguin Group (NZ), 67 Apollo Drive, Rosedale, North Shore 0632,
New Zealand (a division of Pearson New Zealand Ltd)
Penguin Books (South Africa) (Pty) Ltd, 24 Sturdee Avenue,
Rosebank, Johannesburg 2196, South Africa
Penguin Books Ltd, Registered Offices: 80 Strand, London WC2R 0RL, England

Designed by Jasmin Rubero
Text set in Chaloops
Manufactured in China on acid-free paper

5 7 9 10 8 6 4

Library of Congress Cataloging-in-Publication Data
DiPucchio, Kelly S.
Gilbert Goldfish wants a pet / by Kelly DiPucchio ; illustrated by Bob Shea.
p. cm.
Summary: Gilbert has everything a goldfish could want except a pet of his own, but none of the animals who come
near his fishbowl seem quite right until Fluffy, with his long tail and whiskers, appears.
ISBN 978-0-8037-3394-7 (hardcover)
[1. Goldfish—Fiction. 2. Fishes—Fiction. 3. Pets—Fiction. 4. Animals—Fiction. 5. Humorous stories.]
I. Shea, Bob, ill. II. Title.
PZ7.D6219Gil 2011
[E]-dc22
2010028806

To any outsider, Gilbert had everything a
goldfish could ever want.

A **magnificent** stone castle.

A treasure chest **full of gold.**

And a feast of **tasty flakes** that fell from the sky just in time for breakfast each day.

But the one thing Gilbert did not have
was the very thing that he most desperately wanted:

A pet.

Sometimes he imagined his pet would be small.

Sometimes **big**.

Sometimes **really** BIG!

Sometimes Gilbert imagined
his pet would have fur.

Or feathers.

Or floppy ears.

But every day
and always,
Gilbert imagined
what it would be like
to have a pet
to care for and love.

Then one day,
Gilbert woke up to
find a dog barking at him.

BARK!

BARK!

BARK!

Gilbert blinked his eyes to make sure he wasn't dreaming.

The dog wagged his tail and licked the bowl.

Gilbert swam around and around in happy circles.

The dog ran around and around in happy circles too.

"A pet!" Gilbert glubbed. "I have a pet!"

The dog barked.

And barked.

And barked some more.
BARK! BARK! BARK!
Gilbert never dreamed his pet would be so noisy. . .

. . . or so thirsty.

A week passed.

A very tired Gilbert woke up and
the **barky-bark** dog was gone.

The castle was quiet again.

Gilbert was just a teensy bit relieved.

A few days later, Gilbert noticed a small gray mouse peering at him through the glass. Gilbert's little fishy heart went pitter-**patter-swish.**

The mouse licked her paws and sniffed the bowl.

Gilbert swam around and around in happy circles.
The mouse, who thought Gilbert was a large
chunk of cheddar cheese, ran around and
around in circles too.

"A pet!" Gilbert glubbed happily.
"I have a quiet pet!"

The mouse sniffed.

And sniffed.

And sniffed some more.

Sniff. Sniff. Sniff.

When the hungry mouse determined that Gilbert
was not, in fact, a block of cheese,

she ran away.

And she never came back.
Gilbert's little fishy heart went **pitter**-patter-plop.

More time passed and Gilbert had just about given up
on his dream when a fly landed on the rim of his bowl.

"Well, hello there, little fellow!"

Gilbert called out cheerfully.

The startled fly
buzzed around
in circles.

Buzz. Buzz. Buzz.

Gilbert jumped up and the wide-eyed fly was there
to greet him in midair!

"A pet!" Gilbert glubbed.
"I have a quiet, friendly—"

TH WACK!

Oh, my.
Poor fly.
And poor Gilbert.

He cried enough tears to
fill a ten-gallon aquarium.

In the morning,
Gilbert opened his eyes.
Somebody was watching him.
Gilbert gulped.
Somebody flicked its long tail and wiry whiskers.

Gilbert cautiously swam
around and around in circles.
Somebody followed.

Gilbert jumped.

Somebody jumped too.

Hmmm, Gilbert thought, eyeing the curious
new creature before him.

Not too loud. Not too rude. And not too squished!

"A pet!" Gilbert glubbed. "I have the perfect pet!"

"You look kind of hungry," Gilbert said.
"Would you like to join me for breakfast?"

The creature moved in closer . . .
and closer . . .
and closer . . .
and then it took a **BIG** bite . . .

. . . of a delicious green flake.
"The pink ones are really good too,"
Gilbert said with a smile.

"Would you like me to show you around the castle?"

Now Gilbert really does have everything
a goldfish could ever want.
Including a pet.
Fluffy!